The Secret Garden

Frances Hodgson Burnett

Adapted by
Mary Sebag-Montefiore

Illustrated by Alan Marks

Reading Consultant: Alison Kelly
Roehampton University

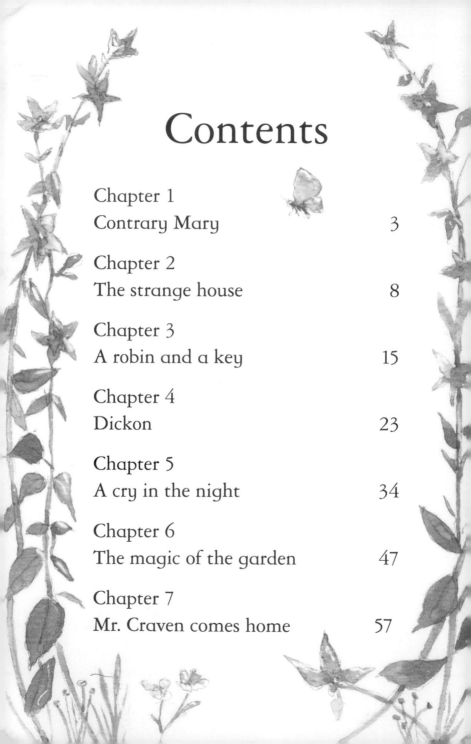

Contents

Chapter 1

Contrary Mary

In the scorching heat of a garden in India, Mary Lennox stamped her foot. "Fetch me a drink NOW!" she ordered.

Instantly, servants rushed to obey. Meanwhile, Mary began to make a pretend garden, sticking flowers into the hot dry earth.

"It looks all wrong," she muttered.

Glancing up, Mary saw a beautiful woman strolling past, surrounded by an admiring group of army officers.

"Mother!" cried Mary. She rushed forward, but Mrs. Lennox brushed her daughter away, as she always did.

It was Mary's last glimpse of her mother. Over the next few days a terrible fever, cholera, swept through her parents' house.

Her mother and father died, along with many of their servants.

Mary, shut away in the nursery, never caught the cholera. But she was left all alone in the world.

After that, Mary was passed around like a package between her parents' friends, until a letter came from her uncle, Mr. Craven.

Dear Mary,

I have made arrangements for you to come to England and live at Misselthwaite Manor. My housekeeper, Mrs. Medlock, will meet you in London and escort you here.

I'm afraid I won't see you for some time as I have to travel to Europe on business.

Yours sincerely,

Archibald Craven

"No one cares what I want," Mary thought, but she had nowhere else to go.

Chapter 2

The strange house

Several weeks later, Mary was
sitting in a cold carriage, opposite
the stern-looking Mrs. Medlock.

"What's that whooshing noise?"
Mary asked, as they drove across a
bleak landscape.

"It's the wind howling across the
moor," Mrs. Medlock replied.

"What's a moor?" asked Mary.

"Miles of empty land – and the
manor is right in the middle of it."

"I hate it already," thought Mary.

"How many servants will I have?" she asked.

Mrs. Medlock looked shocked. "I don't know how it was in India," she said, "but here you'll take care of yourself."

They arrived late at night. Mrs. Medlock marched Mary across a huge hall, up steep stairs and along twisting corridors.

"Your bedroom," she announced, at last, flinging open a door. "You must stay here, unless you're going outside. On no account must you go poking about the house."

As soon as Mary stepped into the room, Mrs. Medlock shut the door and hurried off.

Mary looked around. It was not
a child's room. Tapestries hung on
the walls and in the middle stood a
vast four-poster bed.

Outside the wind howled like a
lonely person, as lonely as Mary.
Then another noise pierced the
wind – a far-off sobbing sound.

"That's not the wind," Mary thought. "It's a child crying. Who is it?"

She was itching with curiosity, but she didn't dare disobey Mrs. Medlock. Finally, worn out from her journey, she fell asleep.

Chapter 3

A robin and a key

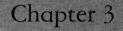

The next morning, Mrs. Medlock
bustled into Mary's room with
her breakfast.

"Ugh!" exclaimed Mary, looking
at the porridge. "What's that? It
looks disgusting. I won't eat it."

15

Mrs. Medlock sighed at the pale, skinny child, swamped by the big bed. "Just drink your milk then," she said, "and you can go out."

"Don't want to," retorted Mary.

"Well, if you don't, you'll be stuck in here and there's nothing to do inside," snapped Mrs. Medlock.

Mary took a while to get dressed – she'd always had servants to dress her before – but finally she was ready.

Mrs. Medlock showed her the way to the gardens and she wandered out, past wintry flower beds and trees clipped into strange shapes.

The only person she could see was an old man digging.

"Who are you?" demanded Mary.

"Ben Weatherstaff," he growled.

"What's in there?" Mary asked, pointing to a crumbling, ivy-covered wall behind them.

"Ah," said Ben. "That's the secret garden. Mr. Craven shut it up."

"Why?" asked Mary.

Ben looked sad. "It was Mrs. Craven's special garden and she loved it. But she died and the master was so unhappy, he buried the key and went away."

As he spoke, a robin flew up to Ben. His wrinkled face creased into a smile.

"There's no door," Ben went on, "but that doesn't stop this one."

The robin cocked its head to the side and looked at Mary. Enchanted, she whispered, "Will you be friends with me?"

"So..." Ben murmured. "You can be friendly. You sound just like Dickon talking to his animals."

"Who's Dickon?" asked Mary.

"He's the brother of a maid here," said Ben. "Dickon can grow flowers out of stones and charm the birds. Even the deer love Dickon."

"I wish I could meet him!"

But Ben was growing impatient. "Run along now," he said. "I've got work to do."

The robin flew off. Mary followed him. "Please, robin, show me the way to the garden," she begged.

The robin chirruped and hopped up and down on the ground.

"He's telling me something," thought Mary. She scrabbled in the soil and saw, half-hidden, a rusty ring. Picking it up, she saw it wasn't a ring at all. It was a key.

It's the key to the secret garden!

Chapter 4

Dickon

Every morning, Mary
jumped out of bed, ready to
search for a way into the garden.
"I have the key," she told herself.
"I just need to find the door."

Mrs. Medlock noticed a change in her. "She looks downright pretty now, with her rosy cheeks," she thought. "She was so plain and scrawny at first."

One day, as the winter trees were beginning to blossom and the wind came in sweet-scented gusts from the moor, the robin fluttered down and hopped along beside Mary.

Mary never knew if what happened next was magic. A gust of wind lifted up a patch of ivy to reveal an old wooden door. Mary put her key in the lock, turned it with both hands and pushed. Slowly, the door creaked open...

She was inside the secret garden!
It was a mysterious place – a
hazy, frosty tangle of rose branches
that trailed the walls and spread
along the ground.

Hundreds of green spiky shoots
thrust up through withered grass.
"It isn't completely dead,"
she whispered. "I am glad."

The shoots looked so crowded that she began to clear spaces around them. The robin chirped, as though pleased someone was gardening here at last.

Mary worked for hours. "It must be lunchtime," she thought, hungrily. "I'd better go in, before Mrs. Medlock starts looking for me."

Racing back after lunch, she noticed Ben talking to a curly-haired boy, with a fawn by his side. As the boy walked away, he played a tune on a rough wooden pipe.

Shyly, Mary went up to him. "Are you Dickon?"

"I am," he grinned. "And you're Mary. Ben told me about you."

He looked so friendly and kind,
Mary felt she could trust him.
"Can you keep a secret?"

Dickon chuckled. "I keep secrets
all the time. If I told where wild
animals live and birds make their
nests, they wouldn't be safe."

"I've found the secret garden,"
she said quickly. "I think it's mostly
dead. I'm the only person who
wants it to live. Come and see."

She led him through the ivy
curtain and Dickon looked around,
amazed. "I never thought I'd see
this place," he murmured. "It's like
being in a dream."

31

He scraped a rose branch
with his pocket knife. "There's
green underneath," he said.
"These roses are alive.
Some dead wood needs
cutting, that's all."
Mary danced
around the garden
in delight.

"It'll be a fountain of roses, come summer," said Dickon. "We'll add more plants too – snapdragons, larkspur, love-in-a-mist. We'll have the prettiest garden in England."

"Will you really help?" asked Mary. She could hardly believe it.

"Of course," he replied. "It's fun, shut in here, waking up a garden."

Chapter 5

A cry in the night

Every day they worked in the
garden. "I don't want it too tidy,"
Mary decided. "It wouldn't feel like
a secret garden then."

"It's secret, sure enough" said Dickon. "Look – the robin's building a nest. He wouldn't do that, unless he felt safe."

"I feel safe and happy here, too," Mary confided. "But I used to be angry all the time. Nobody liked me."

Dickon's fawn nuzzled Mary's hand and he laughed. "There's someone who likes you," he said. "So does the robin and so do I."

That night, lying in bed, Mary heard the wind rage.

"I don't hate it now," she realized.

She thought of the wild animals on the moor, snuggled in their holes, protected from its blasts.

Suddenly, she was alert, listening.

"There's that noise again," she thought. "Crying. It's not the wind. Where's it coming from?"

Gripping her bedside candle, she followed the sound down shadowy passages, until she reached a door with a glimmer of light beneath.

Quietly, she opened the door. A fire burning in the grate threw a dim light onto a huge carved bed. In the bed was a boy, sobbing. Dark eyes stared from an ivory-white face.

"Are you a ghost?" he whimpered.

"No," said Mary. "Are you?"

"I'm Colin Craven," said the boy.

Mary gasped. "Mr. Craven's my uncle. I'm Mary Lennox."

"Well, Mr. Craven's my father," said Colin.

Mary looked at him in astonishment. "Why didn't Mrs. Medlock tell me about you?"

"I don't let people talk about me," Colin said, "because I'm going to die."

Mary was horrified. "What's wrong with you?"

Colin sighed. "I'm weak."

"You won't die from that," Mary scoffed.

"And my father doesn't even care," Colin went on, as if he hadn't heard. "He hates me because my mother died when I was born. He can't bear to look at me."

"Just like the secret garden," Mary said.

"What garden?"

"Your mother's garden," Mary explained. "Your father shut it up after she died."

"I'll have it unlocked,"
Colin announced grandly.
  "No!" cried Mary.
  "Why not?"

"Then *everyone* would go in it. It
wouldn't be a secret any more!"
  "Never mind," said Colin, fretfully.
"I'll never see it anyway."

"Yes you will!" argued Mary. "You go outside, don't you?"

"Never," said Colin. "I can't cope with cold air. Don't forget I'm dying."

Mary felt he was rather proud of this and she didn't like it. "Don't talk about death all the time," she said. "Think of other things."

Her voice dropped to a whisper. "Think of the sun and rain and buds bursting into flower. Think of new green leaves. Think of the secret garden, coming alive…"

Gradually, Colin's eyes closed, and Mary crept away.

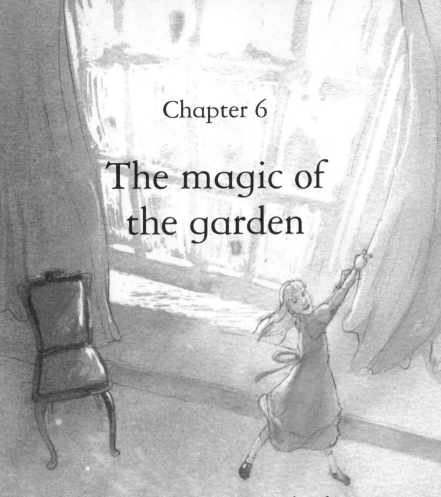

Chapter 6

The magic of the garden

The next morning Mary had to see if she'd dreamed it all. She burst into Colin's room and pulled back the curtains, flooding the room with sunlight.

Colin sat up in bed and smiled.
"I've just realized," he said.
"We're cousins!"

They were talking so loudly they
didn't hear Mrs. Medlock come in.

"I told you not to go poking
around," she shouted at Mary. "Go
back to your room *at once*."

"No," Colin ordered. "I like her.
I want her to stay with me."

"She'll tire you out," said Mrs. Medlock. "Come along, Mary."

"DO WHAT I SAY!" screamed Colin. "Leave Mary and get out."

"Yes, dear," said Mrs. Medlock, trying to sound soothing. She'd promised Mr. Craven she would never upset Colin. Hurriedly, she withdrew.

"You're horribly bossy," said Mary. "I used to be like that, when I lived in India. But I'm trying to change now."

"Why shouldn't I give orders?" snapped Colin. "I'm master of this house when Father's away."

Mary got up to leave.

"Don't go!" pleaded Colin, all trace of bossiness gone from his voice. "I don't want to be alone."

"I'll be back later," Mary promised. "I have a friend I want you to meet."

A few hours later, Mary and Dickon crept into Colin's room.

"You've been ages," complained Colin, scowling at them.

"Say hello to Dickon," said Mary. "I want you to come out with us. I want to show you a secret."

"The garden?" guessed Colin.

Mary nodded.

"I'll come," he decided and rang a bell to summon Mrs. Medlock.

"I'm going outside," he stated. "Bring my wheelchair. And tell everyone to keep away."

"Are you sure, dear?" she asked, anxiously. "You'll catch cold."

"Just do as I say," Colin ordered.

Dickon pushed Colin along the paths until Mary, flinging back the ivy, opened the garden door.

Sunshine lit up sprays of flowers and the air was alive with birdsong.

Colin stared. "I can *feel* things growing," he gasped.

"It's spring," said Dickon. "Makes you feel good. We'll soon have you working in the garden."

"But I can't even stand," Colin faltered, looking at his thin legs.

"Only because you haven't tried," said Mary.

Dickon helped Colin to his feet.

"Try now, Colin. You can walk, you really can," urged Mary.

Unsteadily and clinging to
Dickon, Colin forced his weak
limbs to move. The others saw his
pale face grow rosy in the sunlight.

"Mary! Dickon!" he cried. "I'm
going to get well. I can feel it."

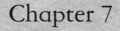

Chapter 7

Mr. Craven comes home

Every day they played and worked in the garden and, every day, Colin grew stronger.

By the time spring turned into summer, he was completely well. But the three of them pretended he was still ill.

"No one must know," Colin insisted. "I want to surprise my father. If only he'd come home..."

Colin began to wish, "Come home, come home."

One night, Colin's father, far away in Italy, had a strange dream. He heard his dead wife calling his name.

"Where are you?" he pleaded.

"In the garden," came the reply, like the sound from a golden flute.

Mr. Craven woke, determined to return to his manor at once.

"Where's Colin?" he demanded, the minute he arrived home.

Mrs. Medlock gasped, shocked at his sudden appearance.

"He plays in the garden, sir, with Mary and Dickon," she said in a shaky voice. "No one is allowed near them."

"In the garden?" thought Mr. Craven. "My dream..."

As he hurried down the path, he heard children laughing in his wife's old garden.

"The door's locked and the key's buried," he told himself. "I must still be dreaming."

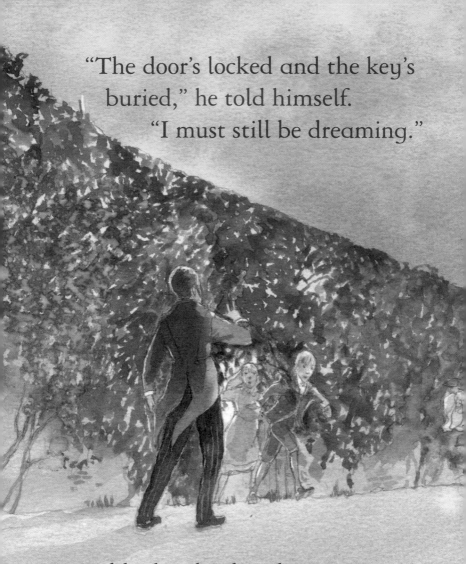

Suddenly, the door burst open and Colin and Mary dashed out. "Father! You're here!" cried Colin.

Mr. Craven hugged his son tight. "Is it really you? You're well! However did it happen?"

"It was the garden," said Colin. "And Mary."

"I thought the garden would be dead," murmured his father.

"It came alive," said Mary.

Mr. Craven smiled. "And so has Colin," he said. "Thank you Mary."

Frances Hodgson Burnett

Born in England, in 1849, Frances moved to
America with her family when she was 16.
A year later, Frances sold her first story. She
went on to become one of the most famous
children's writers of all time. Her other
books include *A Little Princess* and
Little Lord Fauntleroy.

Series editor: Lesley Sims
Edited by Susanna Davidson
Designed by Louise Flutter

First published in 2007 by Usborne Publishing Ltd., Usborne House,
83-85 Saffron Hill, London EC1N 8RT, England. www.usborne.com
Copyright © 2007 Usborne Publishing Ltd.